AF080640

Why Marriages Fail

Bright Mills

Ukiyoto Publishing

All global publishing rights are held by

Ukiyoto Publishing

Published in 2023

Content Copyright © Bright Mills

ISBN 9789360166939

All rights reserved.
No part of this publication may be reproduced, transmitted, or stored in a retrieval system, in any form by any means, electronic, mechanical, photocopying, recording or otherwise, without the prior permission of the publisher.

The moral rights of the author have been asserted.

This is a work of fiction. Names, characters, businesses, places, events, locales, and incidents are either the products of the author's imagination or used in a fictitious manner. Any resemblance to actual persons, living or dead, or actual events is purely coincidental.

This book is sold subject to the condition that it shall not by way of trade or otherwise, be lent, resold, hired out or otherwise circulated, without the publisher's prior consent, in any form of binding or cover other than that in which it is published.

www.ukiyoto.com

Dedication

A very special thanks and acknowledgement to Joshua Becker, Janaina Andrade Tenório Araújo, Albenise de Oliveira Lima, Farid Rusman, for their expertise and assistance throughout all aspects of my research and for their help in writing the manuscript.

About the Book

This book is about problems in marriages, their causes and possible solutions. It discusses the power dynamics in your relationship. While it is okay to have departments that you both look after, it is important to have a fair power distribution. Have you been sitting and wondering why is marriage hard? Have marriage problems made you question your relationship and whether or not it would last? Marriages can be challenging for most people as it involves melding your life and goals with someone else's. Sometimes individuals and couples can feel dissatisfied, unhappy and unfulfilled in their marriages/relationships and be unsure as to what exactly is wrong. There are many factors that contribute to a satisfying marriage/relationship such as; Love, Commitment, Trust, Time, Attention, Good Communication including Listening, Partnership, Tolerance, Patience, Openness, Honesty, Respect, Sharing, Consideration, Generosity, Willingness/Ability to Compromise, Constructive management of Disagreements/Arguments, Willingness to see another's viewpoint, Ability and Willingness to Forgive/Apologise, Fun. The list is simple and obvious yet it can be very difficult for individuals /couples to restore their marriage/relationship to a satisfying one when difficulties arise or when they drift apart. There are many areas of closeness that can enhance a marriage/relationship, help it to remain strong and help it to get back on track when it has become distant/difficult. Sometimes couples feel that things are not right between them, they wonder what is wrong and what they can do?

Contents

Fundamentals Of Marriage Relationships	1
Areas Of Closeness	4
The Faith Relationship	6
The Overlooked Reasons	7
Major Reasons Of Failure In Marriages	11
Factors Contributing To Marriage And Relationship Breakdown	13
23 Marriage Problems And Solutions	17
Case Study 1	27
Successful And Healthy Marriage	28
Case Study 2	32
Separation And Loss: A Study On The Impact Of Divorce	33
Analysis And Discussion Of Results	37
Case Study 3	42
Interpersonal Relationship And Communication	43
Between Husband And Wife: A Case Study	43
In Batu City	43
About the Author	52

Fundamentals Of Marriage Relationships

One of the common marriage problems is when there is a difference in the expression of love. You and your partner do not need to show love in the same way, and therefore, it can lead to misunderstandings. Identify and understand your partner's expression of love. Maybe they have certain things they do by going out of their way, to show their love to you, but because you have a different perspective to it, you do not notice it. Appreciate them when you realize the same. An inequality of power in your relationship or marriage could become a problem in your marriage. Power could be financial or just about the dynamics of your relationship. Discuss the power dynamics in your relationship. While it is okay to have departments that you both look after, it is important to have a fair power distribution. Have you been sitting and wondering why is marriage hard? Have marriage problems made you question your relationship and whether or not it would last?

Marriages can be challenging for most people as it involves melding your life and goals with someone else's. Marriage problems after kids or other major changes can be challenging to deal with and can lead to resentment and feelings of disappointment. Marriage problems, however, are often a result of complacent behavior and oversight. These problems can be resolved with the right approach and openness to reflect. When coming together in marriage, husbands and wives usually develop their own natural, human plan for marital happiness. The couple's separate plans are based on the unique personalities and personal differences of each partner, including different family influences, role models, books, and often-different church experiences. Because their plans for marriage happiness are different, conflict usually results. Since each of us is self-centered, we constantly want to know what our spouse has done for us lately.

Sadly, as time passes, we subconsciously revert to the "greener pasture syndrome" where we begin to compare our spouse's performance with our own pre-conceived ideas and expectations, making satisfaction with our spouse more and more elusive.

Couples fail to anticipate differences resulting from diverse cultural backgrounds, differing family experiences, gender, and so on. Couples buy into the notion of a "fifty-fifty" relationship, meaning they honestly expect their spouses to meet them halfway. Society has taught us that mankind is basically good. Therefore, couples fail to anticipate their self-centered natures that demand their own way. Couples fail to cope with life's trials. When painful trials come into the marriage, instead of standing together through them, couples tend to blame each other or think something is wrong with the spouse and the way they handle the pain. Many people have a fantasy view of love. They quickly feel stuck with an unloving person and become deceived into believing that the next one will be better. Many people lack a vital relationship with Jesus Christ. It could be that they have never come to a specific point in time when they asked Christ into their lives and therefore He has no impact on the marriage relationship.

Sometimes individuals and couples can feel dissatisfied, unhappy and unfulfilled in their marriages/ relationships and be unsure as to what exactly is wrong. There are many factors that contribute to a satisfying marriage/relationship such as; Love, Commitment, Trust, Time, Attention, Good Communication including Listening , Partnership, Tolerance, Patience, Openness, Honesty, Respect, Sharing, Consideration, Generosity, Willingness/Ability to Compromise, Constructive management of

Disagreements/Arguments, Willingness to see another's viewpoint, Ability and Willingness to Forgive/Apologise, Fun. The list is simple and obvious yet it can be very difficult for individuals /couples to restore their marriage/relationship to a satisfying one when difficulties arise or when they drift apart. There are many areas of closeness that can enhance a marriage/relationship, help it to remain strong and help it to get back on track when it has become distant/difficult. Sometimes couples feel that things are not right between them, they wonder what is wrong and what they can do?

The following four areas of closeness can help guide a couple in assessing how their relationship is and can also guide a couple in how to become closer and improve their relationship when difficulties arise, or when they have become distant from one another.

Areas Of Closeness

Doing things Together

Physical Closeness

Emotional Closeness

Sexual Closeness

None of the four areas above is more important than each other but each can help another area to thrive and all together, they can help a relationship become more satisfying, closer, and more intimate

Doing Things Together

It is important that couples spend time together. With busy lives, many commitments and children to care for couples can find themselves with very little time for each other. Spending time together regularly, shopping, dining out, going to the cinema, walking, swimming, involvement in sports, exercising, sharing hobbies and holidays can help couples become closer and have more time to talk and therefore get to know one another better.

Physical Closeness

It is important for a couple to be close physically. This can include eye contact, holding hands, hugging, sitting close together, massaging one another. More opportunities for physical closeness will enhance a couple's sense of closeness and intimacy. It is important for couples to be conscious that some individuals are more comfortable being physically demonstrative than others and it is important to try to understand how comfortable or otherwise your spouse/partner is and take it from there.

Emotional Closeness

Emotional closeness will help couples get to know and understand each other more deeply and also have empathy for each other. It involves being open with each other about feelings, thoughts, beliefs, values, hopes, worries, fears, dreams and ambitions. Attentive listening enhances emotional closeness when both individuals listen in order to get to know and understand their spouse/partner more fully, rather than to disagree, judge, blame oror criticise their spouse/partner.

Sexual Closeness

It is important that both individuals are happy with their couple sexual relationship and feel able to raise and discuss their sexual relationship with the other as needed. Sometimes couples can be very concerned about the frequency of their sexual activity. As long as both individuals are happy with the frequency and the nature of their sexual activity there is no need for them to be concerned or to compare their sexual relationship to those portrayed in the media or those reported by others of their acquaintance, both of which can be at variance with reality.

The Faith Relationship

The faith relationship is opposite of the performance relationship in two significant ways. First, it is not natural at all – it is supernatural. You will only learn about this kind of relationship from God through His Word. Second, the faith relationship does not focus on the human performance of one's spouse but on God's character, promises, and faithfulness. This kind of relationship involves God as the Guarantor of the marriage with the specifics of the guarantee found in Scripture. It's long-term hope based on God's character and faithfulness. We know He is good and loves us. His guidance that led us to marry a certain person becomes more important than the initial human attraction that brought us together. You begin to focus more on Him and His Word, rather than your spouse and his or her failure to perform to your expectations.

When considering the faith relationship, one question that often comes up is, "can God fulfill my needs in this marriage despite my spouse's weaknesses?" The answer is yes! If God can meet your needs anyway, then your spouse's weaknesses no longer limit you. This fact frees husbands and wives to love one another unconditionally as they thank God for His gracious provision. Christ set the example for the faith relationship in 1 Peter 2:21-25. Rather than focus on the failure and weakness of those who unjustly wronged Him, He focused on God and His promises. In 1 Peter 2:23 we read, "but (Jesus) kept entrusting Himself to Him who judges righteously." Jesus believed in God's sovereign plan more than His desire to abandon the cross, more than His disappointment over Peter's denials, and more than His desire for His persecutors to receive instant justice. Christ based His relationships on faith in God rather than the performance of man. Think about how Christ responded to the failures of others on the cross. Could there be a better example for husbands and wives to model in their own marriage?

The Overlooked Reasons

We all know financial problems and poor communication can cause marital problems, but what other threats are lurking in the distance? The statistic that 50% of marriages end in divorce has been highly debated and disputed over the last few years, yet that number just keeps swirling around. It often prolongs younger generations' decision on when or whether to marry. Although the divorce rate varies depending on demographics, it can happen to any couple, and wanting to prevent a permanent parting of ways is a very real concern for most couples. While finances and communication have been cited as some of the most common causes for divorce, we overlooked reasons that marriages fail.

Lack of Investment

We think of investments about money. However, we forget about the time investment and education investment that we need to have in learning how to maintain successful marriages. "Why do we think we don't need any skills when going into a marriage? What other job do we sign up for without any training?" asks Sadler. Sadler's advice includes simply investing time in each other that may include 2-3 hours of your undivided attention for your partner and of course seeking out couples' counseling and/or books to help you navigate the obstacles of a marriage.

Unforgiveness

Our inability to truly forgive our partners in marriage is one of the major reasons that they fail. True forgiveness is when we are able to treat our partners as if the offense never happened which proves to be very difficult for couples. We are constantly reliving the trauma of past experiences which never gives the wounds the opportunity to heal.

Not Showing Up for Your Spouse

So many things can happen in the course of a marriage as Dr. Bradford mentioned. As we experience the ups and downs of life, it's important that our partners "show up," in some of the most difficult experiences whether that's losing a home, the death of a child, or a sick parent. Sadler advises the importance of being able to ask your partner "What is it that you need?" instead of making assumptions. She cites a major issue as the tendency we have to simply want to fix the problem. "Every situation doesn't need to be fixed. Sometimes you just need to show up," warns Sadler. Showing up includes being able to communicate that you may not know what you need at the time, but finding the opportunities to talk through these tough situations and be honest with your partner.

Forgetting the Friendship

Somehow the terms "husband" and "wife" add so much more pressure than we've experienced in our relationships prior to the marriage. Often times, without realizing it, we forget about the friendship that was formed in the dating process and get so far away from it after the nuptials. Sadler advises that we approach marriage with friendship at the forefront and learn to be able to communicate with our partners from a friend perspective without always being so easily offended.

Unspoken Expectations

This is definitely an area that seeps into our ability to communicate but is a very specific part of the puzzle that is often missed. Not only do we ignore an opportunity to communicate our expectations, but we also begin to act on those expectations not being met. We come from different backgrounds and expect different things and never communicate that to our partners. Women never let men know how crucial security is to us. We think men should know to provide, protect, etc., but it is rarely discussed in detail. Men are being brought up in single parent households and have no examples of what it means to be that security, Lack of Flexibility.

Even if a couple has done their due diligence and discussed and agreed on the big topics like finances and parenting styles, there needs to be room in the plans for things to change. A partner's ideas about working outside of the home may change after a child enters the family, or health issues could arise that impact your sexual relationship. I think the key to managing changes that were not expected is to remember that you and your partner are on the same team and should put your heads together to tackle the issue and not each other. If you find it difficult to do this on your own then scheduling an appointment with a couple's therapist may be a great strategy to help you both get some clarity and perspective.

Familial or Societal Pressure

Often times our families have thoughts on who we should marry. Women tend to also be racing the clock when it comes to getting the husband and the family started so they are not marked with the scarlet letter of being "30 something and single. This can lead to making rash decisions in marriage that in turn can lead to divorce. Addressing the pressure that we face as women when it comes to marriage. "At some point, people will understand the danger of living and loving for others to which they will want to leave the marriage. In that case, it may be the best decision for both parties involved. It's never too late to find yourself and most of us need to find ourselves every few years."

Lack of Self-Knowledge

There's a mix of people that never explored what they like or need and there are others that go with what their family thinks is good for them. These people date who looks good on paper for the family and for a societal image. Whether this is to fit in or stand out, depends on the individual and their life experiences. My advice to overcome this is to take your time getting to know and love yourself. Understand what you like and do not like. Document how situations make you feel and if you are able to overcome them quickly or not. Talk your feelings out with your partner, friends or a therapist so you do not internalize emotions. Finally, accept that you will change over time. What you like at 25 may not be what you like at 30 and that's okay."

Major Reasons Of Failure In Marriages

Some marriages can be saved with communication and work. When the marriage cannot be saved, we guide wives and husbands through the divorce process. Often divorce disputes can be settled amicably – through divorce collaboration or mediation. When divorces cannot be settled, we fight to secure your financial fortune and to guide you through the anxiety of divorce.

Failing to share responsibility for raising the children

Raising children includes a lot of joy but also a lot of work and a lot of money. Constant communication is needed to decide which parents will make sure the child is fed, attends school, develops a moral sense, enjoys healthy social relationships, and much more. Parents need to continually attend school events, review their children's homework, answer the child's questions, and much more. Raising and disciplining children should be the responsibility of both parents. When one parent feels the other parent is not making the proper contributions, resentments can form. Frustrations can linger. When the child's needs are not being met, a parent may feel that divorce is the only way to force a solution.

Postponing problems instead of discussing them

Relationships involve daily decisions about a variety of issues such as the activities of the day and the chores to be done. Long-term decisions such as what each spouse wants with their career are a part of marriage. Spouses need to find the time to ask about the concerns of the other and to discuss their issues openly. When problems continually get passed down the road, one spouse may feel that all hope of communication is lost.

An unsatisfactory sex life

Some sexual problems can be resolved with communication. Many times though, the marriage just does not have the romantic and intimate spark it once did. The desire to be intimate is gone. When the fire simply is not burning, many spouses decide that the marriage should end.

Spouses who develop new relationships or rekindle old ones

When a spouse reconnects with an old girlfriend or boyfriend or is intimate with a non-spouse, a serious breach of the marital contract has occurred. Some couples can come to terms with an outside relationship. Many couples cannot. The injured spouse feels they have no choice but to dissolve the marriage and hire a family lawyer.

Financial problems

One additional cause, not discussed in the Huffington Post articles, is financial difficulty. If one spouse is earning a living and the other isn't, then the working spouse may feel the need to end the marriage. A spouse who sacrifices a career to raise the children may fee she/he is being taken for granted. Sometimes, even when both spouses are working there isn't enough to money to pay the bills. If one spouse has a costly addiction or an inability to handle money that too can force the end of a marriage.

Factors Contributing To Marriage And Relationship Breakdown

Unemployment and work related problems

A discernible and quite striking trend noted in submissions was the importance attached to unemployment and other work related issues as factors contributing to marriage and relationship breakdown. Many submissions, particularly from welfare organisations suggested that the pressures placed on family life from unemployment are great and have a strong impact on the well being of relationships. Unemployment not only has the effect of causing financial hardship but also lowers self esteem, creates isolation and limits the ability of families to lead fulfilling lives in the community. Similarly, at the other end of the spectrum, other families, due to financial pressures and fear of losing employment, are working longer hours with a consequent reduction in time for family. This in turn places additional stress and pressure on family life.

Comments included:

Poverty associated with lack of adequate employment is a pressing issue. Unemployment, underemployment and the changing nature of paid work from full time permanent toward casual employment all contribute to reduced financial security, lowered expectations, isolation and disharmony for some families. Families are faced with increasing pressure from this changing nature of paid work. These uncertainties limit the ability of families to purchase homes, have access to credit or lead fulfilling lives in the community. This pressure has a strong impact upon the well being of their relationships.

Many families struggle with poverty, unemployment or the uncertainty and fear of unemployment. Children growing up in such families frequently have lower expectations of stable economic futures. Financial strains are a major factor in family breakdown.

Families are spending less time together and the inability of various family members to communicate effectively with each other is an outcome of this. This is exacerbated by some employers who refuse to recognise that workers have family responsibilities. The difficulties which couples face in dealing with social pressures can exacerbate relationship problems. For example, the economic demands of long periods of unemployment can prove too great for some. Work practices which are 'family unfriendly' can reduce the ability of couples to resolve differences. The pace of change, combined with high levels of uncertainty about the future of jobs etc. can be very destabilising.

High risk factors

In many submission it was argued that the existence of certain factors in marriages place relationships at a high risk of breakdown. For example it was suggested that marriages often break down largely as a result of problems associated with alcohol, drugs and gambling. Apart from the economic drain they cause, such addictive behaviours, often bring associated problems of domestic violence. Illness was also cited as creating destabilising stresses within families. For example, children with a disability, or chronic or life threatening or psychiatric illness within families were also reported as having a negative impact on marital stability. As the Tasmanian Premier's Office said, statistics indicate that the potential for relationship breakdown is likely to follow the birth of a child with severe disabilities or the sudden death of a child or infant. Adelaide Central Mission suggested that another group of families which is particularly vulnerable to relationship breakdown is the group of blended families where there are children from previous marriages. Couples often lack understanding of the complexity of issues they need to deal with, and have unrealistic expectations. These marriages are statistically at high risk of breakdown. Marriage and relationship breakdown in the family of origin was also cited in some submissions as placing marriages under more stress. People who spend their developing life experience in a dysfunctional family may not be equipped to establish and maintain a healthy, happy, ongoing relationship.

Cultural themes

In terms of cultural issues, a strong theme coming through submissions is that the redefinition of gender roles has had a major impact on marriage and the family. In the wake of the Women's Movement, women now have a radically new view of their role and status in society and many men are still uncertain how to respond to this change. Submissions on this theme came from a diverse range of groups and included the following comments: Economic factors and the rights of women to choose to work have changed the dynamics of relationships over the past 20 years. Role models provided by parents are not always relevant roles for the current generation where more women need to work. The influence of the feminist agenda of equality has made the style of relationships change. The traditional roles of earlier generations have become more diverse with several styles of relationships. Conflict and breakdown may occur when one or the other partner changes and the other does not understand how to renegotiate their role within a relationship. The rapidly changing status of women and the resultant demands on men being aspects of social changes to which many people have not adjusted, particularly in relation to concepts of marriage. The current patterns of marital breakdown is caused by the fact that the basic personal and cultural norms of gender are changing. However there is little preparedness on men's part, for a conscious accommodation to changes on the part of so many women. Changing roles of both men and women have challenged expectations of marriages and lead to uncertain and unrealistic divisions of labour within families. The greater participation of women, then married women and finally married women with dependent children in the paid work force has had widespread ramifications for fertility, expectations of marriage and the roles of men and women in relation to their family responsibilities. Some proponents of radical feminism have been quite hostile to the institutions of marriage and family feminism sees divorce as a liberation from an oppressive institution, not a break up of a sacred trust.

Individualism

Several submissions suggested that many couples enter marriage believing that individual rights and needs should override the good of the marriage partnership. Such couples, it is argued, have been poorly trained or equipped for a lifetime of commitment. 22 They often have unrealistic exceptions of the challenge of marriage and the media images of blissful relationships contribute to high expectations without necessarily the concurrent skills.

Parenting

A lack of parenting skills was cited by some social welfare groups as placing stress on families. Organisations such as Marymead and Home-Start Australia argued that the child rearing years are some of the most stressful and couples approach parenting with little or no preparation. There are often few supports to deal with this and no longer are extended families available to support young parents. It was also suggested that the time when children reach adolescence is a very demanding time for many parents, and relationships may be under threat due to these associated pressures. One submissions further suggested that the trend toward adult children remaining longer in their family of origin and third generation unemployment also created added stress on families.

23 Marriage Problems And Solutions

There are many common problems in married life, and many of them can be avoided, fixed, or resolved using many different methods and techniques. Take a look at the most common marital issues married couples face, and learn how to solve marriage problems before they cause irreparable damage to your relationship.

1. Infidelity

Infidelity is one of the most common marriage problems in relationships. The most recent data suggests that about 20 percent of interviewed men admitted to cheating on their partner compared to 10 percent of women. It includes cheating and having emotional affairs. Other instances included in infidelity are one-night stands, physical infidelity, internet relationships, and long and short-term affairs. Infidelity occurs in a relationship for many different reasons; it is a common problem and one that various couples are struggling to find a solution to. Solution: How to fix marriage problems pertaining to infidelity? Infidelity can happen when the connection in your relationship is not strong and can cause a breakdown of trust. Research reveals that maintaining a strong emotional bond, sexual intimacy, and respecting boundaries are the three key ways to combat infidelity in your relationship.

2. Sexual differences

Physical intimacy is indispensable in a long-term relationship, but it is also the root cause of one of the most common marriage problems of all time, sexual problems. Sexual problems can occur in a relationship for several reasons paving the way for subsequently more marriage problems. Studies reveal that sexual compatibility, along with sexual satisfaction, was cited as the most crucial factor in determining relationship satisfaction for couples. The most common sexual problem within a marriage is a loss of libido. Many people are under the impression that only women experience issues with libido, but men also experience the same. In other instances, sexual problems can be due to the sexual preferences of a spouse. One person in the relationship may prefer different sexual things than the other spouse, making the other spouse uncomfortable. Solution: Communication and keeping an open mind are key to getting through any form of sexual incompatibility. It can reestablish the crucial physical and emotional bond for sexual intimacy to flourish.

3. Values and beliefs

Certainly, there will be differences and disagreements within a marriage, but some differences are too significant to ignore, such as core values and beliefs. One spouse may have one religion, and the other may have a different belief. Differences in values may lead to an emotional chasm, among other common marriage problems. As you may have guessed, this could cause significant trouble when one spouse gets tired of doing things separately, such as going to different places of worship. Such marriage problems are widespread in cross-cultural marriages. Other differences include core values. These include the way children are reared and the things they were taught during their childhood, such as the definition of right and wrong. Since everyone does not grow up with the same belief systems, morals, and goals, there is much room for debate and conflict within the relationship. Solution: The only solutions to conflicts arising from different values are communication and compromise. And in matters where compromise isn't possible, the best solution is to be understanding and agree to disagree on these matters.

4. Life stages

Many people do not consider their life stages when it comes to a relationship. In some instances, marriage issues occur simply because both spouses have outgrown each other and want more out of life from someone else. Growing apart with time is a common issue among married couples who have a significant age gap, whether it is an older man and younger woman or older woman and younger man. Personalities change with time, and couples might not remain as compatible as they once might have been. Couples with an age difference who are in different phases of life face this common marriage problem. Solution: Take regular stock of your relationship to ensure that you and your partner grow together and do not grow apart with time. Try to love and accept the different changes that life brings for both of you individually and as a couple. Another thing to try out is an activity. Try to pick up new hobbies that give you both a chance to rediscover each other and develop your bond.

5. Traumatic situations

When couples go through traumatic incidents, it adds more challenges in marriage. Traumatic situations are other problems that couples may experience. A lot of traumatic events that occur are life-changing. These traumatic situations become problems for some married couples because one spouse does not know how to handle the situation at hand. One spouse may not know how to function without the other due to being in the hospital or on bed rest. In other situations, one spouse may require around-the-clock care, causing them to be solely dependent on the other spouse. Sometimes, the pressure is too great, and the responsibility is too much to deal with, so the relationship spirals downward until it comes to a complete end. Solution: Take a break! It might seem selfish, but your relationship can benefit from you taking some time to process your feelings. A therapist can help you or your partner through any traumatic experience and give you the tools to help you deal with these challenges.

6. Stress

Stress is a common marriage problem that most couples will face at least once within their relationship. Many different situations can cause stress within relationships and instances, including financial, family, mental, and illness. Financial problems can stem from a spouse losing their job or being demoted from their job. Stress from family can include children, problems with their family, or the spouse's family. Many different things trigger stress. How stress is managed and handled could create more stress. Solution: Stress within a relationship needs to be handled, or it can destroy the relationship. You can try to resolve this issue by talking to each other honestly and patiently. If talking doesn't help, you can try to take up hobbies like yoga or meditation that help you deal with your stress better.

7. Boredom

Boredom is a severe but underrated marital problem. With time some spouses become bored with their relationship. They may get tired of the things that occur within the relationship. In this situation, it comes down to being bored with the relationship because it has become predictable. A couple may do the same thing every day without change or a spark. A spark usually consists of doing random things from time to time. If a relationship lacks spontaneous activities, there is good chance boredom will become a problem. Solution: Do the unexpected. Whether it is in the bedroom, or other areas of life, to get rid of the boredom in your relationship. Surprise your partner with a gift, an unexpected plan, or some new sexual move, and watch your relationship transform.

8. Jealousy

Jealousy is another common marriage problem that causes a marriage to turn sour. Being with them and around them can become a challenge if you have an overly jealous partner. Jealousy is suitable for any relationship to an extent, as long as it is not overly jealous. Such individuals will be overbearing: they may question who you are talking to on the phone, why you are talking to them, how you know them and how long you have known them, etc. Having an overly jealous spouse can strain the relationship; a lot of stress will eventually end such a relationship. Solution: The only remedy for excessive jealousy is self-reflection to address insecurity effectively. If this is hard to do on your own, you can also take the help of a psychologist who can help you or your partner understand the reasons for your jealousy and how to minimize it.

9. Trying to change each other

This common relationship problem occurs when couples overstep their partner's boundaries to mold their beliefs. It does happen that such disregard for your partner's boundaries might happen by mistake; the extent of retaliation from the spouse that is being attacked is usually appeased in time. Solution: Don't just love your partner, but also learn to respect their boundaries and not force them to change. If you face difficulty accepting certain things about your partner, try to remember that you fell in love with your partner as they are, and so did they.

10. Communication problems

Sad couple in kitchen. Lack of communication is one of the most common problems in marriage. Communication encompasses both verbal and non-verbal cues, which is why even if you have known someone for a long time, a slight change in the facial expression or any other form of body language can be misunderstood. Men and women communicate very differently and can fall into a habitat of improper communication. If such relationship or marriage issues are allowed to fester, then the sanctity of marriage is definitely at stake. Healthy communication is the foundation for success in marriage. Solution: Harmful communication patterns can become a habit, and the only way to remedy them is to make a conscious effort towards improvement. Little by little, you can learn healthy ways of communicating that enhance the relationship and the individuals equally.

11. Lack of attention

Humans are social creatures and are avid seekers of attention from others, especially those closest to them. Every marriage, over time, suffers a common relationship problem, 'lack of attention,' where a couple, intentionally or unintentionally, redirects their attention to other aspects of their lives. Lack of attention changes the chemistry of marriage, which instigates one or the spouse to act out and overreact. This problem in marriage, if not dealt with appropriately, can then spiral out of control. Solution: Listen to your partner, first and foremost. You can also try to take up a couple's activities like dancing or hiking, which can help you give attention to each other in a refreshing new way. It can help you tune out the noise of daily life and genuinely focus on each other.

12. Financial issues

Nothing can break a marriage faster than money. If you are opening a joint account or handling your finances separately, you will encounter financial problems in your marriage. It is essential to discuss any financial issues as a couple openly. Solution: Finances can be a sensitive topic, and couples should carefully discuss these problems. Try to come up with a plan that meets your shared financial goals. Also, try to make sure that the motivation is discussed openly if someone deviates from the plan.

13. Lack of appreciation

A lack of gratitude, recognition, and acknowledgment of your spouse's contribution to your relationship. Your inability to appreciate your spouse can be detrimental to your relationship. Solution: Try to appreciate all that your partner brings into your life. Leave them a surprise note, or you can give them a flower or spa couple, just to show your appreciation. If you are the one who feels undervalued in the relationship, try to communicate this to your partner. Without blaming them or making them feel cornered, express your feelings and need for change. Your honest feelings might make them realize their oversight and compel them to make changes.

14. Technology and social media

The emerging dangers of social media on marriage and family are imminent. With a rapid increase in our interaction and obsession with technology and social platforms, we are moving further away from healthy face-to-face communication. We are losing ourselves in a virtual world and forgetting to love other people and things around us. Such fixation has quickly become a common marriage problem. Solution: Reserve an hour each day or one day a week when you and your partner go technology-free. Keep your phones and other devices away to try and focus on each other without any distractions.

15. Trust issues

This common marriage trouble can rot your marriage from the inside, leaving no chance of restoring your relationship. The idea of trust in a marriage is still very conventional and, at times, puts too much strain on a marriage when the doubt starts to seep into a relationship. Solution: With the assistance of a therapist, open communication can help a couple understand the reasons for their mistrust and ways that they can resolve them. The therapist could also suggest some trust-building exercises to help you learn how to trust each other.

16. Selfish behavior

Even though selfishness can be efficiently dealt with by making minor changes in your attitude towards your spouse, it is still a widespread marriage problem. A big part of being in a relationship is melding your life with another person and their priorities. Couples often find this transition difficult as collective priorities can clash with personal ones, which can cause problems. Solution: Empathy is the only solution for selfish behavior. Try to understand each other's perspectives and make being considerate a habit. If your individual goals are at odds with your goals as a couple, try to talk to your partner with open vulnerability.

17. Anger issues

Losing your temper, shouting or screaming in rage, and causing physical harm to yourself or your spouse is sadly a common marriage problem. With increasing stress due to internal and external factors and in a fit of rage, we might be unable to control our anger, and an outburst towards our loved ones can be very harmful to a relationship. Solution: If anger is an issue you struggle with, consider talking with a counselor to learn coping skills to help keep anger at bay so it doesn't affect your relationship. You can also start by counting to ten before saying angry words that might ruin your relationship.

18. Keeping score

When anger gets the best of us in a marriage, a widespread reaction is vengeful or seeking retribution from your spouse. Keeping count of battles won and lost within a relationship can set the foundation for an unhealthy relationship. It would make you want to settle the score constantly and lead to resentment. The priority then becomes having the upper hand rather than being there for each other. Solution: Keeping scores is for sports, not relationships. You can learn to deal with marriage problems by learning not to keep a count of who got their way in fights and disagreements. Focus on the bigger picture and let go of the small battles you might have had to compromise.

19. Lying

Lying as a common marriage problem isn't only restricted to infidelity or selfishness; it also comprises white lies about day-to-day things. These lies are many times used to save face and not let your spouse get the high ground. Couples might lie to each other about the difficulties or problems they might be facing at work or in other social scenarios; such marriage problems burden a relationship. When things get out of hand, it can very much wreck a marriage. Solution: Analyze the reasons why you or your partner feel compelled to lie instead of being honest. Only once to understand and address these reasons can you attempt to end the lying and dishonesty in your relationship.

20. Unrealistic expectations

Have you been sitting and wondering why is marriage hard? Have marriage problems made you question your relationship and whether or not it would last? Marriages can be challenging for most people as it involves melding your life and goals with someone else's. Marriage problems after kids or other major changes can be challenging to deal with and can lead to resentment and feelings of disappointment. Marriage problems, however, are often a result of complacent behavior and oversight. These problems can be resolved with the right approach and openness to reflect.

21. Ignoring boundaries

While it is okay to point out certain things that your partner can improve about themselves, it may not be the best idea to pester them into changing too much or overstepping boundaries they have set. This can become a marriage problem if not checked in time. Solution: Discuss boundaries. Let your partner know if you want a night out with your friends every two weeks. Explain the concept of boundaries if they have problems understanding the idea. Help them set healthy boundaries for themselves, as well. Respect their boundaries, too.

22. Emotional infidelity

Infidelity can be of various types. However, the one that mostly comes to light is physical infidelity when a partner has physical relationships with one or multiple people outside the marriage or relationship. However, emotional infidelity is when a partner develops romantic feelings for someone other than their partner. Emotional infidelity can also become a marriage problem since feelings for someone else can damage your marriage or relationship.

Solution: If you start to develop feelings for another person, check yourself. Introspect to see what these feelings mean.

23. Division of labor

Are the chores in your marriage divided equally or fairly? If not, it can become a big problem in your marriage. Solution: Not to sound repetitive, but really communication is the key. Talk to your partner about the chores, how you feel about them, and how you can divide the chores between the two of you.

Case Study 1

Successful And Healthy Marriage

"Success in marriage does not come merely through finding the right mate, but through being the right mate."

– Barnett R. Brickner

Years ago, my family and I embraced a minimalist lifestyle. We decided that too much clutter had collected in our home and it was demanding too much of our money, energy, and precious time. We embarked on a journey to sell, donate, recycle, or remove as many of the non-essentials possessions from our home as possible. It was one of the best decisions we ever made. When we began removing the "stuff" from our life, we found a whole new world open up. We found that we had more time for the things that we valued most. Now, as a result, we spend more time at the dinner table, we take longer walks as a family, and we have been able to save money for some worthwhile experiences—like a weekend at the beach, for example.Removing the non-essentials has allowed us to focus more on the essentials. And we have discovered that true life is found there. Often times, our marriages follow the same trajectory. At first, when we have nothing but each other, we focus intently on the important building blocks of a healthy and successful marriage. But as our relationship continues forward, "stuff" begins to accumulate and begins to distract us from the very essentials of what makes a good marriage.

Suddenly, we worry more about the appraisal value of our home than the value of our relationship. We check the health of our retirement account far more often than the health of our marriage. Or we spend more time taking care of the car in the garage than the other person in our bed. Things begin to accumulate in our homes and lives and soon demand our money, energy, and precious time. As a result, we have little left over for caring for the very elements of a happy marriage. Wise couples realize that a nice home, car, or retirement account may appear nice to have, but they do not make a successful marriage. They understand that there are far more important principles at play. They have learned to invest their money, energy, and time into the 8 essentials of a healthy marriage:

1. Love/Commitment.

At its core, love is a decision to be committed to another person. It is far more than a fleeting emotion as portrayed on television, the big screen, and romance novels. Feelings come and go, but a true decision to be committed lasts forever—and that is what defines healthy marriages. Marriage is a decision to be committed through the ups and the downs, the good and the bad. When things are going well, commitment is easy. But true love is displayed by remaining committed even through the trials of life.

2. Sexual Faithfulness.

Sexual faithfulness in marriage includes more than just our bodies. It also includes our eyes, mind, heart, and soul. When we devote our minds to sexual fantasies about another person, we sacrifice sexual faithfulness to our spouse. When we offer moments of emotional intimacies to another, we sacrifice sexual faithfulness to our spouse. Guard your sexuality daily and devote it entirely to your spouse. Sexual faithfulness requires self-discipline and an awareness of the consequences. Refuse to put anything in front of your eyes, body, or heart that would compromise your faithfulness.

3. Humility.

We all have weaknesses and relationships always reveal these faults quicker than anything else on earth. An essential building block of a healthy marriage is the ability to admit that you are not perfect, that you will make mistakes, and that you will need forgiveness. Holding an attitude of superiority over your partner will bring about resentment and will prevent your relationship from moving forward. If you struggle in this area, grab a pencil and quickly write down three things that your partner does better than you—that simple exercise should help you stay humble. Repeat as often as necessary.

4. Patience/Forgiveness.

Because no one is perfect (see #3), patience and forgiveness will always be required in a marriage relationship. Successful marriage partners learn to show unending patience and forgiveness to their partner. They humbly admit their own faults and do not expect perfection from their partner. They do not bring up past errors in an effort to hold their partner hostage. And they do not seek to make amends or get revenge when mistakes occur. If you are holding onto a past hurt from your partner, forgive him or her. It will set your heart and relationship free.

5. Time.

Relationships do not work without time investment. Never have, never will. Any successful relationship requires intentional, quality time together. And quality time rarely happens when quantity time is absent. The relationship with your spouse should be the most intimate and deep relationship you have. Therefore, it is going to require more time than any other relationship. If possible, set aside time each day for your spouse. And a date-night once in a while wouldn't hurt either.

6. Honesty and Trust.

Honesty and trust become the foundation for everything in a successful marriage. But unlike most of the other essentials on this list, trust takes time. You can become selfless, committed, or patient in a moment, but trust always takes time. Trust is only built after weeks, months, and years of being who you say you are and doing what you say you'll do. It takes time, so start now—and if you need to rebuild trust in your relationship, you'll need to work even harder.

7. Communication

Healthy marriage partners communicate as much as possible. They certainly discuss kids' schedules, grocery lists, and utility bills. But they don't stop there. They also communicate hopes, dreams, fears, and anxieties. They don't just discuss the changes that are taking place in the kid's life, they also discuss the changes that are taking place in their own hearts and souls. This essential key cannot be overlooked because honest, forthright communication becomes the foundation for so many other things on this list: commitment, patience, and trust—just to name a few.

8. Selflessness.

Although it will never show up on any survey, more marriages are broken up by selfishness than any other reason. Surveys blame it on finances, lack of commitment, infidelity, or incompatibility, but the root cause for most of these reasons is selfishness. A selfish person is committed only to himself or herself, shows little patience, and never learns how to be a successful spouse. Give your hopes, dreams, and life to your partner. And begin to live life together. This is a simple call to value our marriages, treat them with great care, and invest in them daily. Accomplishing the marriage advice listed above will always require nearly every bit of yourself—but it so worth it if you want to learn how to have a happy marriage. A successful and healthy marriage is more valuable than most of the temporal things we chase after with our lives. And will always last longer.

Case Study 2

Separation And Loss: A Study On The Impact Of Divorce

Abstract

This article emerged starting of a search that had as aimed to understand the feelings that emerge in men and women when they lose marital bond. It was carried under a qualitative basis and counted on the participation of three men and four women, all divorced. The tool used was the semi-structured interview and the collected data was submitted to the Thematic Content Analysis. This analysis led to the conception of two categories: the emerging emotions and feelings in the loss context due to the divorce and the repercussions of such loss about the personal identity. The results indicated that searching and establishing a new affective bond was a strategy used by the participants involved in the study, in order to strengthen and support the resignification of their personal identity. The majority of the interviewees earned such resignification by becoming independent and capable of developing their own potentialities. About the feelings and emotions lived through the critical period of separation; they ranged from "happiness and peace" to "failure and sadness"

Divorce is a relating theme in contemporary times, approached by various fields – legal, social, psychological, economic – since its incidence accompanies the changes that new forms of conjugal currently have. Therefore the individuals experiencing marital untying present significant individual changes, which allow a new meaning to their individual identities. However, reaching this stage can be a slow and contentious process. It is even possible that some people do not reach this stage of inner subjectivity that promotes the meeting with them, becoming thus unable to severance of marital identities constructed in marriage. In this context, the unlink is a process that is influenced by various psychosocial variables, installing tensions in modes of life of the separate subjects. However, to speak in loss of the marital bond, we must first report to the marriage. Whereas the transformations of contemporary, with regard to the requirement of equality between the sexes, the need for preservation of individual liberty among peers, and the coexistence of redistribution of power between the roles of man and woman, we agree with Gomes and Paiva (2003), when they view marriage today, linked to a notion of reciprocal, transformation, flexibility in relation to new and different, providing a space for in- terpersonal development and creativity. Continuing in the same line of reasoning, Féres-Carneiro and Diniz Neto (2010) state that the marital relationship begins with the creation of a common territory in which they begin to be shared experiences that produce patterns of social interaction significant for the couple, relativized by the experience of psychosocial construction of each individual. To these joint experiments, these authors call marital identity. We understand how Féres-Carneiro (2003), that marital identity is constructed through interactions established between the spouses. In this context, based on the marriage of passionate love, being together is no longer sure of the durability of the union, so widespread in other times. This reality highlights the possibility of divorce, and refers to the spouse's searches conjugality that supply their feelings of emptiness and loneliness. Thus, men and women seek partners in order to be happy and put their hope, longing to find, in many times in their romantic relationships, satisfaction hitherto not achieved (Paiva, 2009). In addition, that results in most cases, in separations from dissatisfaction generated by the non-realization of the idealized marital quality. In the separation process, marital identity is slowly crumbling, leading the spouses to a redefinition of their individual identities (Féres-Carneiro & Diniz Neto, 2010).

Typically, the separation occurs in stages. Matarazzo (1992) features six stages: 1) the emotional divorce, when there is an emotional remoteness, revealing feelings such as anxiety, sadness, guilt and detachment; 2) physical separation, when the proximity and physical contact are intolerable, generating feelings of rejection and even hatred; 3) geographical separation; when in fact there is a change of residence; 4) family separation, the relatives are informed that the relationship has reached a moment of weakness and that the only way out is divorce; 5) social separation when the permanence of friendship is shattered and some friends are removed from the social environment, seeking for freedom, bringing with them new friendships; 6) legal separation, when the couple de- termines the division of assets, custody of children at this time can be a process of revenge and denial, or there may be a friendly and conciliatory break. These steps may occur in non-sequenced or more than one of them simultaneously, with each couple in a singular process. By separating the individual can open a new path, a chance to resume their activities way, be they emotional, professional or social; and, with these opportunities come along understanding of being alone in this new process of searching for new significations. Step by step, the dissolution of marital identity will promote a redefinition of the identities of the individual partners. Individual identity in this context follows what Singly quoted by Féres- Carneiro (1998), appointing as the possibility of the individual constitute itself as an autonomous, satisfying their needs for growth and development under optimal and individualistic contexts that stimulate the realization of their projects and desires. In other words, this process arise significant individual changes, which allow the encounter with oneself.

It is this quest for new projects that inserts the newly divorced in new and different social, economic and emotional contexts, we wish to emphasize. Based on the scenario presented, the present study aimed to understand the feelings that emerge in men and women when divorce, lose the marital bond; as also to ascertain the impact of separation on redefinition of individual identity.

Method

This research presents the characteristic exploratory and descriptive, whereas the proposed objective followed the design of qualitative research.

Attendees

Three men and four divorced women, sex, age, religion, education and various socioeconomic backgrounds, all residing in the same city.

To preserve confidentiality of documents and identities of each participant, their real names were replaced with fictional names. The inclusion criterion was to have at least two years divorced. The number of participants was determined by saturation, meaning that this number was considered closed when new interviews began to show an amount of repetitions in content (Turato, 2003). The criterion for selection of the participants was purposeful type, also called an intentional or deliberate. The study was submitted to the Ethics Committee on Research with humans, the University who welcomed the project, Process No. 172.323. Only after their approval, the researcher went to call them to participate in the research. From the first contact with the participants, were marked dates and times convenient for the interview. That day, when the person invited to participate accepted, was signed the Statement of Informed Consent.

Instrument

The instrument used was a semi-structured interview with open questions concerning emotions and more frequent feelings in divorce, as well as questions relating to the impact of separation in their lives, allowing the verification of the resumption of individual identity. The interviews were individual and conducted in a proper environment and convenient to the interviewee. They were recorded – with the permission of the participant – having an average duration of 40 minutes. The data collected after the interviews were analyzed based on three basic procedures constituting the Thematic Content .

Analysis. The first is called pre-analysis, involving a brief reading of the collected interviews. The second is called exploratory, seeks to explore the material, content encoding and adding the thematic units. The third, called the treatment of the results, is characterized by the development of interpretations and syntheses. The definition of thematic units was prepared in advance, depending on the objectives of this research. Was elected two units, namely: 1. Emotions and more frequent feelings; 2. Impact of separation on the redefinition of individual identity.

Analysis And Discussion Of Results

Emotions and Frequent Feelings

A striking aspect of the process of separation between the former spouses is the possibility of developing a symptom of grief, where feelings of disappointment and heartbreak are present, making this moment a traumatic event that promotes emotional destabilization. This data is a source of difficulty in the study subjects, both in terms of talking about feelings experienced after separation; as to express the pain and sorrow that involves loving untying. For example, at the beginning of the interviews appeared expressions such as: "is reviving talk about it"; "this matter is still painful." The interviewees' statements showed feelings of jealousy mixed with the shame of being separated; depression accompanied by apathy and isolation; sense of dislocation and difficulties to face the new civil context:

I was jealous at times, I was ashamed at other times as well (Marcelo, engineer, 31 years old, divorced for nine years). Feelings of depression of being isolated and not wanting to go to work anymore. I spent a week without going to work (John, teacher, 28 years, divorced for two years). I kind of lost, I think I got trauma, a trauma in my life (Priscilla, seller, 49 years old, divorced for five years). Even after two years and five months, the sadness still. There is still a disappointment, hurt, wounded. The trauma exists, but gets lighter (Ana, nutritionist, 30 years, divorced for two years). However, in some situations, the feelings that come with the rupture are freedom, happiness and relief. Consider talking to other interviewees: Freedom, ah! Was the best feeling I've never been so happy in my life than in those early years of separation, God! (Jacqueline, university professor, 47 years old, divorced for 10 years). Then I went to have freedom, is the right word, freedom to do what I wanted: to dance, play! That is when I started playing, going out. After I divorced him, I was to be happy! I was really happy to be! (Renata, housewife, 58 years, divorced for 10 years)

Despite expressions of pleasure contained in these statements, Porchat (1992) warns us that even experiencing these feelings contrary to pain and suffering, nobody gets immune to a marital separation. There are conflicting and opposing vibrations between relief and despair; breaching is always a situation of pain and emotional affectation, regardless of who takes the initiative or who only suffers the action of untying. Jacqueline, for example, in the continuation of the interview tells us that, despite having taken the initiative to divorce, is currently unable to establish a more lasting bond because it fears experiencing the failure of the marriage again. As Renata, lived a marriage marked by her husband's infidelity and embarrassment of seeing him making use of alcohol what resulting her feeling of freedom after divorce. However, today, Renata not allows her new relationships for fear of repeating "mistakes of the previous relationship" (Sic). In summary, in the separation process all the feelings and emotions are experienced intense and confrontational way. They vary according to the roles assumed during the divorce, create difficulties in performing daily activities and promote emotional instability.

Impact of Separation on the Redefinition of Individual Identity

From the departure of a marriage, there is an exit that Bucher-Maluschke (2003) calls "we married" for the resumption of individual identity – a subjective process, which presents significant individual changes. This recovery is not linear; it is loaded with internal tensions that interfere in the ways of social, economic and psychological actions of newly divorced. The interferences that separation brought social life experienced by respondents were, at first, as unpleasant, triggering feelings of displacement: The first outputs, you feel like a duck out of water, you were already used to having that person next to you (Ana). I went back to my parents' house where I felt better (John). I felt lost and at the same time, having to find me, I cannot explain, it is really deep, it's too difficult and complicated (Priscilla).

The feeling of displacement may be stronger for some people and, in turn, trigger compensatory excesses that lead to loss of the reference point indicating to them the way forward: I had a great social change after separation. I began spending every day with the staff of the university to have a beer and do what is not worthy (Marcelo). In this Marcelo' speech fragment is visible his escape mechanism in relation to love loss. Anton (2005) states that the subject realize that is not the target of the affections of another, suffers an intense sense of loss that resembles brought by death. In the interviews was observed the presence of this feeling reported by Anton, reaching hinder the process of redefinition of personal identity: Today I feel alone, extremely depressed, I miss a company, but I do not dare to relate to anyone (Jacqueline).

We believe that after the deconstruction of 'we marriage' there is an internal reorganization that configures the reconstruction of individual identity. It is the search for new projects, which inserts the newly divorced in new and different social, economic and emotional contexts, that we wish to emphasize now: After the divorce I started doing my friendships, I began to take courses, cookery and confectionery. But I did well was when I started making money, because before I depended of him (Renata). In the professional did not change, but rather the social, I already have links friendships, I already feel good about going out alone (Ana). After we broke up, the first thing I wanted to do was put an end in everything. To give you an idea, on a Saturday I sold a car and a bike that I had, because I did more walking, everything that reminded me that I was married, I wanted to give an end (John). Some participants needed to rebound financially to be able to attain individual reframing: So I went through difficulties for not having an education and had to start all the professional life, I was homeless, lived by rent too complicated, I suffered more so by not having a structure (Priscilla). In the financial I have not difficulties because I've already kept the house financially. Financial impacts came later on account of wage flattening because I started paying pension to him (Jacqueline). Jacqueline's speech goes against what the literature says. By having a better salary than the ex-husband is that she assumes the post-divorce pension.

Finally, in the final phase of redefinition of individual identity, interviewees speak for themselves with a significant improvement in self-esteem, leading them to the feeling of freedom for new bindings: That's when I joined the gym to work out. I wanted to lose that belly, I no longer wanted that belly, I was not 78 years old, I wanted to get muscle mass, I went to an academy (Carlos). Six months later I had a lot more health, was practicing sports, much slimmer, much higher self-esteem (Marcelo). And recently, I'm dating again, and my life is in this way, I do not know if I can be alone, I think I must have someone talking and saying something (John). The new affective investment to John has been responsible for the rescue of the meaning of his life. The absence or presence of a professional psychology to support this transition phase was highlighted by respondents. Let's look at some of the speech: When I talk about this subject, I see I did not look for any professional. This search might have helped me; I think it was something to be solved (Ana). Today I'm another person; I learned a lot from the psychologists who helped me at this stage (Carlos).

Final Considerations

As stated earlier, this research aimed to understand the feelings that emerge in men and women when, divorce, lose the marital bond; as also to ascertain the impact of separation on redefinition of individual identity. Considered to have achieved these goals in time we realize that the feelings and emotions – both positive and the negative – are present in the interviews. Among the positives are the feelings of freedom, happiness and peace. However, the negative evidence of feelings of inadequacy, jealousy and anger mixed with sadness and failure, confirming the literature on the subject.

We also found that the presence of a loving family support contributes to face the moment of marriage breakdown, becoming one of the strategies used for the redefinition of individual identity. On this point, we observe that the search and the establishment of a new affective bond was a strategy employed by the subjects to serve in support of this "reframing". Most respondents won the redefinition of their individual identity, managing to become autonomous and able to develop their individuality. All experienced the process of subjectivation, which promoted contact with them and, from that, succeeded in winning individual, significant changes, marital deconstructing identities and opportunity to the emergence of individual potential. They created existential projects capable of contributing to the uniqueness, growth and maturation of themselves, and being with the other. The respondents moved from dependency to emotional and financial independence, which led them to respect, respecting others and develop in interaction processes. This study advances on previous research and offers new contributions to knowledge currently available on the subject. In this sense, singular and important factor in our study was the care of one of the interviewees with the former spouse, leading to the residence of the former couple in the same house after divorce. In this case, the former spouses have passed through the stages of family, social and legal separation. However, for economic reasons, they kept their houses under one roof, i.e. not implemented the geographical separation. Since the literature has not addressed for this agreement between divorced, we leave it as a suggestion that the formation of this new family arrangement can guide the new research.

Case Study 3

Interpersonal Relationship And Communication Between Husband And Wife: A Case Study In Batu City

Abstract

Family is an important institution in human's lives, and the relationship between husband and wife is essential as it shapes the quality of the individual development. In this case, interpersonal communications also significantly influence the quality of the relationship between husband and wife. This study uses a qualitative approach in the form of a case study. It involves six informants consisting of 3 couple who have been married for at least 25 years. The study seeks to understand how informants build interpersonal communication with their spouses. The data is collected through intensive interviews and analyzed using a descriptive method. Keywords: interpersonal relationship, communication.

INTRODUCTION

Generally speaking, marriage is understood not only as a part of a natural phenomenon but also a cultural construction. Therefore, the development of marital relationship among humans can be different from one community to another, since it is connected to cultural context. Even the marital relationship that develops from one spouse can be different from another since it is closely related to the development of the cultural context of each individual. Marriage cannot be seen merely as biological needs or reproduction– ability to reproduce offspring – to keep the continuity of human species on earth, but also act as a social activity. When marriage is viewed from the social context, it will interact with social and religious values that exist within a particular society. Thus, it will be a part of the culture among a group of people (in a broader context) and especially be a part of the culture within a family (as a smaller social unit).

It is believed that there is interdependency between the quality of family and the quality of society where the family belongs. The better the quality of a particular society, the better the families will be generated. In addition, the better the quality of families, then the better the development of the society will be. In this case, a marriage institution involves not only a relationship between two individuals who agree to marry but also the relationship among other married couples and the society where the marriage institution belongs. Giddens stated that the family is the basic social unit of civil society. As an essential part of society, the social resilience of a society is also determined by the social resilience of families within the group. In other words, when there are more marital breakdowns, then the society where the families live will be more vulnerable. A marital breakdown can happen not only to families with financial pressure but also to those who are financially stable or prosperous. The number of divorces significantly increased during the end of the 20th century in most western countries. Giddens suspected that the number is even higher outside those countries. He specifically stated that the proportion of single-parent families and children who were born from unmarried parents gradually increased. In 1994, 32 percent of birth happened outside marriage in England, 35 percent in France, 47 percent in Denmark, and 50 percent in Sweden. Fukuyama added that 30 percent of White People in The United States of America were single-parent around the same year. As society is exposed by news (and issues that develop within the communities) about marital breakdowns (even divorces) among spouses, either young or old, a study on this area is worth conducting to help people maintain their marriage. The results of this study are expected to reveal the truth behind the success of a marriage as well as ways to develop and maintain the relationship and resolve conflicts within the marriage. Furthermore, the study can be used to unveil how relationship and communication between husband and wife can bring comfort to the children, and contribute to creating and developing healthy society, which has a positive impact on individual well beings. Indeed, marital problems are not limited to the high number of divorces in most parts of Indonesia, including Batu City, but include qualitative aspects inside the marriage, which affect spouse's happiness and children's development. Such aspects require deep understanding and good communication between husband and wife. Thus, this study aims to examine this matter and try to figure out communication models suitable for the cases.

THEORETICAL FRAMEWORK

Communication that includes two individuals which lead to interpersonal communication can be studied using several theories. The researcher begins with the Social Penetration Theory, as stated by Altman and Taylor. The theory divides interpersonal communication into three different stages of relationships; Orientation Stage in which individuals engage in small and simple talks (Colleague), Exploratory Affective Stage which individuals start to reveal the inner self bit by bit (Friend), and Affective Stage in which individuals feel more comfortable talking about personal matters (Best Friend). The three stages of relationships mark the breadth and the depth of communication that can be seen from the communication topics. The breadth of communication involves the range and variety of topics, while the depth is related to whether or not the topics include private or personal matters. The beginning of the relationship is often marked by the narrowness and the shallowness of the topics. If the relationship develops into a more intimate one, then the breadth and the depth of the topic will increase.

On the Orientation Stage where individuals become "Colleague," the topics will only cover public

information and not a personal one, such as general profile. Also, the materials of the discussion do not vary. As the relationship moves to a deeper stage as "Friend," the communication material will include one's preference on food, clothes, music, even aspiration, and ambition. Besides, the discussion topics in this stage will be more varied compared to the previous one. As it goes deeper to the next stage of becoming "Best Friend," the communication materials will include private matters, such as self-concept, religious belief, emotional situation, and so forth. This kind of relationship involves more variety of discussions compared to the others.

Therefore, it is crucial to understand that the stages of "Colleague," "Friend," and "Best Friend" are actually interwoven. Altman and Taylor stated that the relationships are not always getting better; sometimes, it is decreasing and even ended. In the marital communication context, it is possible for either husband or wife to treat his/her partner as "friend" or "best friend." Another theory is the Social Exchange Theory from Thiboult and Kelley. It states that interpersonal communication happens since there is hope in each individual to obtain advantage from communicating with others. Griffin stated that the initial background of an individual to communicate is similar to utilitarianism philosophy, which views human acts based on utility. Each individual realizes that communication requires cost, yet it is expected that the result will gain more than the cost. The fundamental value of this theory is the gain loss principle, which resembles the trading principle.

When a person assumes that his/her communication does not gain anything, then he/she will slowly decrease the intensity of communication and eventually stop. On the other hand, the person will continue the communication if he/she still hopes to gain profit. As Fitzpatrick is interested in individuals' point of view on each partner on marriage, Eric Berne focuses on personalities shown by a person to his/her partner. This theory – also called game theory – divides human personality into three categories, namely "Parent State," "Adult State," and "Child State". The Parent State is marked by a tendency of "lecturing," "thinking of being more understanding than others," "protecting," "spoiling," and so forth. The "Adult State" shows the tendency of "being rational," "being firm," and "being disciplined. The "Child State" is more on "being emotional," "wanting to be spoiled," "being dependent," etc.

Furthermore, individuals usually play a specific role in communicating with their partners. In some cases, a wife plays a role as "child" and the husband as "parents. This communication completes each other since they divide the roles. Additionally, the relationship pattern tends to be in harmony because they need each other. This is qualitative-descriptive research in the form of a case study involving three couples. It examines the relationship and interpersonal communication that develop among couples. The subject of the research was three married couple (six people) who had been married for at least 25 years. They were selected using quota sampling. The 25 years of marriage or more is considered adequate to be used as a study material. Data were collected through in-depth interview and free-talk, especially interpersonal interview with each person without the involvement of the partner. The in-depth interview was a discussion where the researcher took control of the material or topic, while the free-talk was further discussion between the researcher and the research subject. During the free talk, both parties (the researcher and the research subjects) had an equal chance to choose issues to be discussed.

The data analysis was performed since the beginning of data collections and continued as the researcher wrote the report. Generally, the data were analyzed descriptively to depict the relationship and interpersonal communication between husband and wife.

RESULT

As previously mentioned, the research involved three different marriage cases. The three cases and the findings are described below. Case I: The first couple, Ahmad Wahyudi (husband) and Sumiyati (wife), had been married for 26 years. Ahmad Wahyudi found it surprising that his wife was not as romantic and sweet as she had been when they were still dating. As time went by in togetherness under the marriage vow, Wahyudi tried to accept the fact about the changes in his wife's attitude. He realized that his wife also faced an unexpected outcome on marriage, the truth that the marriage life was far from what she expected. It made him try harder to make his wife happier in the marriage. He tried to improve the quality and quantity of his communication with his wife. Thus, in the 5 years of marriage, they succeeded in having two sweet children. They also successfully solved the problem that occurred in the early days of their marriage life. From Sumiyati's point of view, Wahyudi had disappointed her.

However, later, she understood that marriage life is the real life that they had to face, and it was different from when they were still dating as two young adults. She learned more about her role as a wife for her husband and a mother for her two children who had finished higher education and now had a job. Her relationship with her husband experienced the dynamics of harmony and conflicts, which were mostly caused by economic or parenting problems. Sometimes she felt that her husband was her good friend while other times she thought of him as a stranger, even as an enemy. However, she acknowledged that the quality of the communication between a husband and a wife defined the condition of their relationship. Case II: The second couple, Bambang Pujo (husband) and Fitriyani (wife), had been married for 25 years.

Bambang is a worker in a town government office. He admitted that his relationship with his wife started when they dated for three years before finally taking the relationship to a "more concrete" one, as he called it, which was a marriage life. Because of this, he did not feel that his wife was a stranger when they lived together for the first time as a family. He also admitted that at the beginning of the marriage, their relationship was not as romantic as when they were still dating. He saw differences in the way they talked from when they were still dating to when they were already married. After the marriage, communication tended to be more practical and realistic. There was also some difference in the dynamics of the relationship and communication. He expressed that there were often more serious and complex problems in marriage. Fitriyani, whose daily activity is running a small store because all three of the children are now living independently, admitted that in the early days of their marriage, she experienced confusion. However, she eventually understood that married life was indeed different from dating. Her husband's guidance had helped her to overcome her confusion in facing the condition.

They had made their mind to continue their relationship to the next phase, from dating to a wedding, and they understood the consequence of it was to learn to build the strong relationship in marriage through good communication, which corresponded to the relationship status. She and her husband agreed to keep improving the quality of the communication. When there were problems with the communication between them, she took it as "the colors" of their marriage life. Hence, she believed that the relationship between a husband and a wife that sometimes includes quarreling is normal.

Case III: The third couple, Didik Sudarto (husband) and Ernawati (wife), have been married for 26 years. Didik works as a fruit seller and has been doing his job since their early married life with his wife. Both of his kids are married and have families of their own, so he lives his life with his wife more easily, unlike when the children were still studying in the university. He did not date Ernawati for long. It was less than a year. Because of this, he felt that he did not have enough time to know each other during the short dating period. In the early days of their marriage, he found many differences between them, starting from the outfit preference, the discipline in praying, to the hygiene. Even though they faced differences, he understood that the sacred vow was a promise and an obligation to keep building the family with his wife. Hence, he tried hard to adapt to his wife. He was grateful because his wife was cooperative to improve situations. As they passed the 6th year of their marriage, the communication between the two ran smoothly. He also said that there were also less tense situation and arguments between them. Ernawati, on the other hand, stated that her husband is a patient man. She said that he is a hard worker, although sometimes he made her feel uneasy because he was not disciplined enough about cleanliness and praying. Both Ernawati and Didik enjoy cooking, and they even have relatively similar taste in food. Therefore, the cooking session in the kitchen can be used as the communication time for her and her husband. She admitted that the communication between them improved when the kids grew up and entered university. The children could help taking care of the house and the fruits. She thinks that she needs enough time to communicate with her husband. Besides the quantity, she understood that quality matters. So far, based on the quantity, she admitted that the time she has to communicate with her husband is sufficient.

CONCLUSION

The dynamics of relations develop in case I, where the relationship between husband and wife resembles the relationship as a "friend" or an "enemy," giving colors to the relationship in the early years of marriage. The pattern of the "parent-child" relationship develops in the second case. The husband often facilitates the role of parents in dealing with wives. While in the third case, the "adult - adult" relationship pattern develops, because both of them manage their business (selling fruits) together so that they are involved more in the same work.

References

Case Study 1
Successful and Healthy Marriage
Joshua Becker

Case Study 2
Separation and Loss: A Study on the Impact of Divorce
Janaina Andrade Tenório Araújo
, Albenise de Oliveira Lima

Case Study 3
Interpersonal Relationship and Communication between Husband and Wife: A case Study in Batu City

Farid Rusman
University of Muhammadiyah Malang

About the Author

Bright Mills

Best selling author Bright Mills is a writer, an engineer and a historian from Nigeria. He has a degree in Information Technology. He is a creative writer and have written so many books in Fiction and non fiction. His books have received starred reviews weekly, library journal, and Book list. He promises to pull heart strings, offer a few laughs, and share tidbits of tantalizing history. His work has been praised by many.

www.ingramcontent.com/pod-product-compliance
Lightning Source LLC
LaVergne TN
LVHW041551070526
838199LV00046B/1912